Her Fake Fiance Cowboy

Carsen Brothers Sweet Clean Western Romance, Volume 3

Marie Richards

Published by Marie Richards, 2021.

HER FAKE FIANCÉ COWBOY

The Carsen Brothers of Sweet Rivers Ranch Book 3
(Sweet Clean Marriage of Convenience Western Romance)
By Marie Richards
Copyright 2021 Marie Richards

ACKNOWLEDGEMENTS

Thank you, Lord, for all my blessings. To my amazing family and friends for your love and support. To my wonderful editors Allison and Jane.

Table of Contents

Her Fake Fiancé Cowboy

War hero Jesse Carsen has sworn off marriage after a history of heartbreak. His life is the ranch now, but he knows he has to fulfill the condition of his late adoptive father's will for him to get married in order to take part ownership of the ranch with his brothers. Will his new fake fiancée heal his heart?

Bella Lovely has been labelled a struggling has-been actress by the tabloids since her absence from the screen to take care of her dying father. Her now ex-fiancé, an A-list movie star, left her for a Hollywood starlet and now they're engaged.

She lost her fiancé, her father, and a place in Hollywood all in the space of a month. Now, she can barely afford to keep her home. But she must make a comeback appearance at a film festival where her ex-fiancé and his new bride will be. She just needs a fake fiancé quick to save face and keep the gossipers from ruining her reputation as undesirable. Who could she turn to?

After his adoptive aunt introduces Jesse to Bella, sparks fly between them. He wonders if his fake fiancée could be his *real* bride one day. Can love really heal *all* wounds?

Chapter 1

Jesse couldn't believe his aunt Sue Mae.

"So you really want me to go through with this too, Sue Mae?" he asked after he finished one of his cattle drives.

His aunt was a charmingly determined lady when it came to getting her way. She also never liked to be called auntie. His adopted brothers and he always called her by her name.

At the Sweet Rivers Church, she was known as Sue Mae to everyone, not Sister Sue Mae like her other church sisters, just Sue Mae.

"Yes, I want you to go through with it too, Jesse. You're not getting any younger. You're in your mid-*thirties*. And you're *still* single."

He didn't need any reminders.

"Your other brothers, Luke and Beau are happily married now, and it's your turn," Sue Mae continued.

"And I'm really happy for them Sue Mae. Trust me, but like I said before, it's not going to work for me."

"And why not, Jesse?"

"I'm not marriage material."

"Oh, now Jesse, you know that's not true. Don't let that horrible ex of yours make you think differently."

"It's not about her."

"Well, of course it is."

His aunt was right. Well, partially right.

The trouble was Jesse had issues. He had issues no one could possibly understand, except maybe his brothers that lived on the Carsen Family's Sweet Rivers Ranch, the largest ranch in

Sweet Rivers, Texas. Jesse, Luke, Beau, Chase, Jake, and Zack, all came back to the ranch to help out their elderly adoptive father, Chet Carsen, when he became ill and could no longer work on the ranch. Chet was a decorated war vet who sustained injuries during the war and could not have kids of his own. So his wife and he, while in their older years, adopted many children from the foster care system to give them a good home and a second chance. A chance for a stable, balanced life living on the ranch.

Jesse, along with many of his brothers, followed in his adoptive father's footsteps and also served their country. Jesse served two tours of duties in Afghanistan. He later moved to New York and did some community work with youth before moving back to Texas.

He loved the ranch. It was his home and it was good for his lungs. His asthma got better when he first came to live there. Unlike the city air, the air on the ranch was pure and clean. Being close to nature and listening to the sounds of roosters in the morning did a lot to relax him compared to the noisy sound of traffic in the city.

And he adored those breathtaking sunsets on the ranch. Those stunning red and orange sunsets over the ranch made his heart sing with joy. Tranquility surrounded him out there in the wide-open spaces. There was nothing like it in the world. Sweet Rivers had the best views to nature's finest. It stole his breath away each and every time. His adoptive father taught him to slow down and appreciate the beauty in the world and appreciate all of God's creatures big and small, take in the sunsets and the sunrises and the way everything worked in harmony on the ranch.

The view he'd wake up to each morning was outstanding with the miles of green grass and trees, farm fences, and small streams that glistened under the sunlight.

Jesse found being close to nature invigorating for his soul.

Yes, life was beautiful on the ranch. And he wanted to stay there forever. There was no way he could leave this ranch. No way on this earth. It was his heart and soul. Yet he knew there was more to life than working on the ranch and enjoying the pretty sunsets and sunrises.

He knew his late father had a stipulation in the will that in order to take co-ownership of the ranch, he and his brothers had to be married. It was his father's way of making sure they honored the family tradition and settled down to build a family that would carry on the ranch for generations to come, sharing the love, setting a good example for others.

But the trouble was, Jesse, like some of his brothers, had what a lot of kids who were adopted had. Attachment disorder. It was hard for him to get attached to anyone, after feeling abandoned by his biological family.

And the one woman whom he thought he could have a life together with, left him and went to Europe. She was now married to someone else. He'd moved back to Texas from New York after that. He'd always blamed himself. He had issues with closeness and that was something you needed in a marriage.

"You know I think I might have someone that's perfect for you," Sue Mae continued.

"Oh, no, Sue Mae. I really appreciate what you're trying to do..."

"But you know there's another reason, right?"

"I know. Chet really wants us to get married before we take ownership of the Sweet Rivers Ranch."

"That's right, Jesse. It's part of his last wishes. You know his will was very specific. Before ownership of the ranch is transferred over to you boys, you all have to be married and settled down. He knows you all want to, but you all got discouraged along the way. I guess it's his way of just making sure you don't give up on love. Besides, it's a family ranch. It's in our motto: *From our family to yours*. You can't all be swinging singles here for the rest of your life."

"But we *are* a family."

"Nice try, Jesse. You *all* have to be married, not just some of you. Besides, you don't want to let your brothers down now, do you?"

"No. You know that's the last thing I'd want, Sue Mae." He thought about it for a moment. His father really knew what he was doing, didn't he? He knew they'd all probably put it off and never settle down if it were up to them.

Family first.

Family was everything.

That was all Dad ever preached about. How God made family for a reason. And the family that prayed together stayed together. He'd gotten out of the church when he moved to New York years ago, but since moving back to Texas things had changed. He'd begun to change his perspective and look at things from a different angle.

He adjusted his cowboy hat. "If I didn't know any better, I'd swear this wasn't even legit."

"You know it's legit, Jesse. A man can put anything in his will."

"Within reason."

"Yes, within reason, but he did make it clear. If you want to stay on the ranch, you need to find a good woman and settle down. You'd make a fine father one day, Jesse. I know it's what you always talked about in the past. You're so caring. And I see the way you are with the kids that come here from the hospital for a trail ride."

His heart sank when he thought of the ill children that would come here for a therapeutic visit with their caregivers. He would love to spend more time with them. He even brought the family's border collie, Cocoa, over for a therapy visit with hospital approval after one of the children in the long-term care facility requested it.

Closeness.

It terrified him to get close to a woman though. That was a whole different matter. He loved the animals on the ranch, the guests, and his family, the ones on the ranch and the church family, but could he commit to a woman for life?

The trouble was, he was fearful it wouldn't work out. His own parents were in an abusive relationship and split up and he ended up in foster care because neither could take care of him. Thankfully he spent time with Chet Carsen and the other foster kids and ended up being adopted like his foster brothers while they were in their early teens. They were proud to take on the Carsen name and the Carsen legend. Everything it stood for.

Love. Honor. Courage. Faith.

Could he have faith that things would work out? Two of his brothers had been determined to never fall in love and vowed to only do a marriage of convenience with a divorce later. Of course, they ended up falling in love with their pretty wives. If only it could work out that way for him.

Failure.

He was terrified of failure, of failing in his relationship. He was terrified of not having what his brothers had. He wasn't exactly lucky in the love department.

Speaking of lucky, he was happy for his brother Beau who found love with his convenient wife, Lucky, an animal rescue shelter worker who ended up needing rescuing herself. And then there was Luke who made a beautiful marriage with Jemma, the woman who started *Jemma's Grant-A-Wish* app to help ill children with their wishes.

Could marriage work for him?

Should he go for it? But then again, what choice did he have?

He couldn't let his family down or the ranch. It was a generational gift.

What was he going to do now?

Sue Mae knew everyone at the church—well, she knew everyone's *business*. She loved to chat with everyone and knew who was alone, who was single or who was newly divorced. She boasted about playing matchmaker to many of the couples there at the Sweet Rivers Church. But could she really play matchmaker for Jesse too?

Would he be the first one to let his late adoptive father down?

Chapter 2

Bella Lovely, former star of the TV show, *Look at You* and the motion picture *Love*, looked aghast at her agent.

"What did you just say?" she asked, incredulously.

"Sorry, Bella. You're old news." Moss Gordon never minced his words.

He didn't exactly have what one would call charisma, but he got work done. It was his agency and he could do whatever he wanted, she supposed. He was an older man in his early seventies who did things his way.

"Old news? What's that supposed to mean?"

"Look, you know how it is these days. Producers want to bet on winners. You know I'm blunt, Bella. I don't sugar coat anything."

Moss barely met her eyes. He fidgeted with some papers on his desk, probably hoping she'd get up and leave. What had she been thinking going there to see him this morning? He hadn't been returning any of her calls.

Sure, she hadn't made the agency any money or commission recently, but that was because she'd taken time away to care for her ailing father as he'd been ill for some time. Her dad had been born with a weak heart and needed special treatment.

In fact, she'd burned through her entire savings paying for his medical bills.

Her dear father had just recently passed away and she'd fallen into a downward spiral, questioning everything.

"Is this about John?" Bella asked candidly. It was her turn to be blunt now.

She knew John and she shared the same agent. He was a top Hollywood actor who'd moved from Texas to Tinseltown and made it big. He'd asked her out one day on the set of her TV show when he was a guest. They were the Hollywood "It" couple for a year until he broke off her engagement and went out with another starlet.

He was overheard at a bar telling a friend of his that Bella was too boring to be with. That didn't help her reputation much. Add that to the fact that her show had been canceled due to low ratings and viewership. She'd really counted on that money coming in every quarter. It helped pay her bills. It was a steady income. TV series were most actors' bread and butter because it was consistent, but again that depended on viewership and ratings, didn't it? Old-fashioned cable TV sitcoms had a hard time competing with social media live streams and reality shows these days.

And right now, it was all about popularity and advertisers paying top dollars.

"Now, you know this is not about John," he said, shuffling some more papers on his desk.

Yep. It *was* about John all right.

She wondered if her ex had something to do with this.

Now, she was supposed to be receiving an award on behalf of her father, a screenwriter who wrote the famous "Love Happens" screenplay for his years of service in Hollywood.

She could not show up to the *Dallas Academy of Film and TV Awards* ceremony without a date!

She didn't want to look as if she'd been all washed up and too boring to be with anyone. She knew that her reputation mattered in the industry.

She didn't have time for social media and didn't have many followers, not like John and his new fiancée Alexis. But right now, she wished them the best, but she also wished herself to get out of this slump.

He'd really done a number on her heart and soul ditching her like that so publicly by being pictured romping around with the actress, Alexis, on the set of his new movie and then coming out and saying that they were getting married.

He hadn't even officially broken off with Bella yet either. She guessed it would have tarnished his rep if the world knew he'd been cheating on her with another woman. So he made it look as if it was official when it wasn't yet.

All this because she didn't have much time for him, going to the hospital every day to see her father and to be there by her dad's side.

When her father went to be with the Lord, she felt empty inside. She needed something, she needed hope. And the one person she thought she could count on left her for another woman behind her back. And now her agent was telling her there were no more roles for her.

Did he even try hard enough?

For some reason, she didn't think so. And right now, she didn't know if she had the energy or strength to fight it. She needed to regain her strength. She prayed to the Lord to give her the strength to deal with this and to find a way out of her slump.

Now what was she going to do?

How was she going to afford her apartment?

How was she going to survive now?

She needed a way out. She needed a lot of prayers.

Her dad used to tell her to trust the Lord's timing, that sometimes prayers weren't answered on your timeline but when the time was right.

But when would that be?

She didn't have much time now. Her bills were due. She'd taken out a loan to help cover her father's medical expenses and the payments were now overdue. She was already behind on her rent.

Oh, Lord. How am I going to get out of this one?

Chapter 3

Jesse and his brothers, Beau, Luke, Chase, Jake, and Zack sat on horseback as they guided the cattle from one pasture to the next on their short cattle drive.

Jesse enjoyed spending time with his brothers out in the sun on the ranch, just as their adoptive father had taught them. It gave them time to focus on things other than his problems. He noticed his brothers Luke and Beau who'd just gotten married were so much happier. They seemed to have a spring in their step which was more than he could say for himself.

Jesse thought about his conversation with Sue Mae earlier. Chet was right to leave Sue Mae in charge to make sure his last wishes were honored. She always was one to keep on top of stuff. Still, he didn't have much time. He loved the camaraderie amongst his brothers. He really wanted to keep this land and to enjoy pride of ownership with his brothers. But where would he find someone soon?

"You seem like you've got the world on your shoulders, bro," Chase said to Jesse.

Chase had been adopted at age twelve by the Carsens, just like Jesse. He'd come to the ranch after Jesse from a foster home.

"Yeah, Sue Mae and I spoke earlier."

"Oh, that. I guess you're next in line to the marriage throne, huh?" Chase teased. He probably knew full well he himself would be next.

Sue Mae was not going to stop until all the boys were married off and in a loving family home.

The ranch was big enough. They had dozens of cabins spread out around, close to the main house. It was a wide open, yet close-knit environment.

The Carsen brothers all looked out for each other.

The brothers all bonded quickly when they spent time on the ranch, learning about taking care of the livestock and the land.

The ranch gave them a sense of stability compared to the turbulent homes they'd grown up in. It was hard to trust at first but Chet had taken them to church and showed them how family and God were important as well as respecting one another.

Ranch life gave them a relaxed living. Yes, it was hard work, but there was something about the peaceful co-existence of all life on the ranch. No politics, no rat race, no backstabbing. Not like what he saw in New York in the corporate world. He was glad to leave all that behind and return home to the Carsen's Sweet Rivers Family Ranch.

It was ironic that the name had family in it. It began like that, but it was the largest ranch in Sweet Rivers and had a little retreat lodge for the occasional paying guest. Many visitors loved to visit to get a taste of ranch life and experience on a working ranch, not to mention the horse-riding trail.

They often had kids from foster homes or long-term care treatment facilities visit on one of their therapeutic trips. He and his brothers loved to show them a good time on the ranch. He often took some of them to the hen house so they could see how eggs were collected.

It filled his heart with joy sharing those experiences, just like how his own adoptive father, Chet, showed him and the boys.

"So do you have someone in mind?" Chase asked Jesse. "Or is Sue Mae going to match you up with someone from her church women's group?" He grinned and shook his head.

"Very funny, bro. I don't have anyone in mind, so I guess she's going to set me up on some sort of blind date. You know how much I'm looking forward to one of those." He resisted the urge to roll his eyes.

"Yeah. Those are fun." Chase gave a mock grimace.

Family.

Family was everything to the Carsens. He really hoped he could find someone like his brothers Luke and Beau to settle down with. He knew he needed to at least find a convenient bride for the sake of his obligation to honor his father's last wishes according to the will, but beyond that, he saw how lucky Beau and Luke got with their brides of convenience turning into real brides for life.

Could he be so lucky?

Chapter 4

"Listen," Moss said to Bella. "You're a nice girl. You just might be able to make a comeback, but you've got to take some good advice."

"Some good advice? Like what?" Bella could not believe she was negotiating with Moss. But right now, she needed to survive. She needed to move forward in her life. And her career needed some resuscitation, big time.

"Bounce back. Everyone loves a comeback story."

She sighed deeply. "Hard to do that when doors are closing in your face."

"Yes, that's true. But that's because you gave up too easily. Your famous fiancé dumps you for a prettier and more popular actress. You slink away into the night…"

"Hey, I didn't just slink away into the night." Though it felt that way for a while when her world seemed so dark during her father's illness and after his passing.

She didn't think she could dig herself out of that distraught frame of mind. But she knew she had to. She had to do it for her father's sake. He wanted nothing but the best for his little girl. Her mother had died when she was born so she didn't know any other family. It had always been her and her father. He'd taken her everywhere with him, showed her the ropes, and how things worked in the industry. They even read books together on the film industry and talked about what made movies and TV shows great. She missed him. He was more than a father; he was like her best friend.

They lived in Texas but flew to California for months at a time to work on projects when work was available.

He'd worked so hard between jobs while things were slow in the industry, putting food on the table and sending her to college to get a good education. And now? She was falling. And she didn't know if she could get back up.

Ordinarily, she never cared what people thought of her. Her father had always told her that the only opinion that mattered was what she thought of herself. Still, it hurt that everyone was trash-talking her behind her back, saying how she let herself go and how she had a great guy and let him slip away.

Well, her father had been very private about his life and his illness and didn't want it to be public and she respected that, so she never did make it known she'd turned down a role to spend time helping her father battle his illness.

But now, she had to pick up the pieces and move forward.

It was hard when you felt as if everyone was against you but then she remembered what her father once told her, "When things get crazy, just do your best and the Lord will bless. The Lord can make a way where there is no way. Even if *you* don't see a way out of your situation."

Her father always told her that the Lord spoke through people sometimes. Was this the case now? Maybe Moss had a good point. Hollywood was all about scripts, wasn't it? It was all about image, expectations. Well, she would make a go of it. She'd turn her life around and get back up on that horse, so to speak.

"Just show up to the Dallas awards ceremony, looking pretty. And..." Moss hesitated for a moment. She could tell he was anxious about something. But what was it? she wondered.

"And what, Moss?"

His cheeks were flamed.

"Well, you know, maybe have a beau on your arm. Show them you've still got it. That you're still desirable."

"Desirable?"

"Listen, Bella, I know it's not fair but that's how the world is. People judge you by what they see. They don't know what you've been through these past months. They just see that you've been hiding away..."

"I haven't been *hiding* away. Not every working actress goes to every single Hollywood party getting snapped by the paparazzi."

"Now *I* know that, and you know that. But *they* don't know that. And the opinion polls have agreed with John. They say you're dowdy. Too plain. You never do fun things. You don't even attend awards shows."

Now that really stung.

Sure, she was an actress. She found drama to be a wonderful form of therapy and outlet for self-expression. She could be someone else, anyone, live vicariously through her awesome captivating characters and display that on screen to the world.

But right now, it looked as if she had another role to play. That of someone who was "desirable" as Moss put it. Or someone who was *employable* in Hollywood more like it.

"The Dallas awards show and film festival is only a few weeks away. Just show up with hot date or better yet, say you're serious, you're engaged."

"Engaged?"

"Yes, engaged. They love those sorts of things. Don't let John pull your image down. I think you're a great gal. It's just that...well, you need a bit of a makeover."

"Now there's nothing wrong with..."

"No, no. Not that kind of makeover. More like an image makeover. Hey, there's nothing wrong with that by the way. Hollywood has been doing that for decades back from the silver screen era. It's all about image. Image is what sells. It sells movies. Could you imagine a star of a movie who people think no one wants in real life? Imagine what it would have done to those A-list stars in romance movies."

"I see your point."

"It's not fair, but it's how it is."

"Yes, but shouldn't we try to change that?"

"It's easier to change it on the inside, don't you think? Right now, we've got to get you some roles."

"So you don't think I'm old news then?"

"I never said that."

"Yes, you did. You said it to me five minutes ago."

"Did I? Oh, well, I must have been talking about someone else. Anyway, other people might think your old news. Bloggers and the media might think you're old news. But you've got to get back out there and show them you've still got it."

"Okay."

"Now, you'll need to be discreet. You can't just go on any dating websites."

"Oh, no. I'm going to ask one of my church sisters."

"Church sisters? Now, wait a minute now."

"Trust me, Moss. Let me take care of that part. I will not be going to any app and swiping right for just anybody off the Internet. I need to be careful. The last thing I would want would be for someone to go to the press and spill the beans that I'm on one of those apps looking for a date."

"Yeah, that's what I just said."

She grinned and rolled her eyes. "Anyway, I trust the people at my church. I'm sure I can find a date. There's this nice elder church sister who's always matchmaking."

"Sounds like a plan. Does she have anyone for me?"

"Moss."

"Just kidding. Anyway, just make sure you let me know. I need to send out press releases and post it on our blog."

Just then his phone rang. He excused himself and picked it up.

He spoke for a few moments. "Okay, I'll let you know what she says."

"Good news," Moss said after his call.

"Good news?" She beamed, leaning forward in the chair.

"Yes. I might have something for you."

Her heart leaped for joy. "You do? What's the assignment?"

"It's a commercial for an anti-aging wrinkle cream."

"What?" Her face fell. Her *spirit* felt wrinkled right now.

"I'm kidding." He laughed. "It's not that bad. It's actually for weight loss. See, that's not so bad now is it?"

"I don't believe this." She shook her head astonished.

"Listen, Bella. I'm trying my best. Take it or leave it. The role is yours if you want it."

"I...I don't know what to say..." She knew it would pay her a good, fixed amount plus possible residuals, but that would be the worst thing she could do for her image. Not to mention the laughingstock she'd be doing weight loss commercials right after her ex left her for a fit, slim model turned actress.

"Just get a beau for the awards ceremony and then I'll spin something for you and see what I can do. I hear that James is looking for a lead for his new rom-com. You know those are huge hits. It's based on that popular novel."

Bella lit up. "I would love to do that lead."

That could give her a cool half million and help clear up some of the medical debts left behind after she'd lovingly cared for her beloved father.

"James, the director, is going to be there at the Dallas awards show and festival. Remember, everyone loves a good comeback. Find a nice guy to take you there. You know it's all about image in this business. Image is everything. You've got to *look* like success, if you want success."

She knew that all too well. But could she find someone at the church to go along with it?

Chapter 5

After Sunday service, Jesse got up to leave, putting on his cowboy hat as he made his way out of the service. He had to return to the ranch to help Chase fix the hinge on the barn door.

Sue Mae approached Jesse with a lovely woman beside her.

"Jesse," Sue Mae said, brightly. "This is…"

"I know who this is." Jesse's lips parted with surprise. "Bella Lovely." He could not believe his eyes.

His face must have lit up and his smile must have spread wider than the ocean, but he didn't care right now. Bella Lovely was standing right there in front of him.

"Nice to meet you," he said, tipping his cowboy hat.

"Nice to meet you too." Bella's voice was silky and smooth and warm.

They shook hands, and sparks flew instantly. He felt a sweet tingling sensation through his body. It wasn't often he felt that way by shaking the hand of a pretty lady like Bella Lovely. But she was…lovely. She was lovely in every sense of the word. Her name really suited her.

He wasn't a cowboy that got starstruck often, but this was an exception. He'd watched her TV show every week when it was on the air.

He'd heard that she attended the Sweet Rivers church once in a while whenever she was in town, but he'd never met her in person before. Truth be told, the Sweet Rivers church was a large congregation. In fact, it was so large they had two morning services. One at nine in the morning and the other at eleven o'clock. So it was common to not see everyone who attended.

Bella was originally from Sweet Rivers but moved away to Hollywood to film her TV series. Unfortunately, it was cancelled after two seasons, but he loved watching the show. And he loved watching sweet Bella Lovely, her voice was so smooth and warm, soothing to listen to, her charm came through the TV and right into his heart. And man, could she act.

She was breathtaking. Not like those skinny model types. She was curved in all the right places, a healthy glow about her. Always smiling and always shining.

He felt as if he'd known her for a while since she'd come into his living room almost every Thursday night when he watched her show.

He also heard about her troubles recently and his heart went out to her. Especially with that creep actor fiancé of hers. He could not believe John cheated on her and ran off with another actress. That man didn't deserve to have her.

He wished he could have hugged Bella to make it all better for her, but right now, he may just have his chance.

He was gushing. Sue Mae looked at them with a grin on her lips. She was clearly up to something. But what else could he say to Bella?

Say something, Silly. Say something. Anything.

Was he really this star-struck?

"Well, I'll leave you two alone," Sue Mae said. "I have to uh...head down to the basement to help out with the refreshments."

"Yes, of course." Jesse could say nothing else.

"Would you like some help?" Bella offered.

"Oh, no, dear. I'll be fine." Sue Mae then left them alone and made her exit.

Jesse thought he caught a wink from Sue Mae's right eye, but he could be wrong. It was probably just his imagination.

Jesse and Bella had a nice little chit chat for a few moments, talking about the wonderful singing by the church choir. They had a guest singer from another church who performed a touching solo of Amazing Grace, and the spiritual hymn really brought tears of joy to a lot of members. He really felt connected to Bella talking about the program.

"Can I get you something from the refreshments booth?" Jesse asked Bella later.

"I'm good, thanks," she said, softly. "Actually, I'd love a latte."

"Well, they don't have any here, but we can go...I mean I can get one from the Sweet Rivers Café in town."

"Oh, I don't want to trouble you."

"Hey, it's nothing. Besides, I could have one myself."

"Sure, that'll be great, thanks," she said, her lips curved with a sweet smile.

They made their way out of the church and into the parking lot. He could see members looking their direction and whispering. The great Bella Lovely and cowboy Jesse Carsen. He could only imagine what they would be saying right now. After all, it was a large town, but it was small enough for almost everyone to know each other. And talk got around fast. But right now, he didn't mind. It wasn't like any of them were attached. Not that he knew of anyway. Besides, she was a member of the church, just like him.

Good thing they each had their own vehicle.

"Let me walk you to your car," he said.

"That's very nice of you. You know your aunt has told me so many wonderful things about you."

"She has?"

"Yes, why does that surprise you?"

"Oh, nothing." Jesse felt heat climb to his cheeks. Why was he feeling this way about Ms. Lovely? He was always a guy in control of his emotions. But not now. This was different.

This was Bella Lovely.

"Nice sermon this morning," he said.

"Yes, it was lovely. Pastor Dave really knows how to preach."

"Yes, he does. And the message couldn't be more needed. Love..."

"1 Corinthians 13:4-5: Love is patient, love is kind. It does not envy, it does not boast, it is not proud. It does not dishonor others, it is not self-seeking, it is not easily angered, it keeps no record of wrongs..." she said, passionately.

"My favorite verse. Well, one of my favorites."

"Me too," she said, brightly. "Funny that. I had it put up in my locker in high school. Everyone thought I was weird."

"You're not weird."

"Thanks. Well, as my father used to say, we live by the word. It's what's kept me going. I have to admit, I haven't been to church as much as I wanted to. Especially in the last few years. But...well, after my father went to be with the Lord..."

"I'm really sorry about that. How are you holding up?"

"Thanks," she said, softly. "I'm good. You know, it's not easy, but as Isaiah 40 says, He gives strength to the weary.

Sometimes we have to keep believing. Keep feeding ourselves, not just physical food but encouragement," she told him.

And he was impressed. He didn't often hear people talking so boldly and knowing all the scriptures like that.

"Wow, you really surprise me. I never expected you to...well..."

"I know, based on the roles I've played in Hollywood. Well, it's a job, a career, and I love the art of communication on the big screen, but that's my work. *This* is me. I leave my job at work. Dad always told me to never lose my faith, no matter what I do in life," she said, sadness filled her beautiful large brown eyes. And right there and then, he wanted to hold her.

He could only imagine what she must be going through, losing her father like that and her fiancé in a short space of time and then having a TV show that was cancelled.

He had expected her to look down or depressed, but she seemed so hopeful, so strong, so determined. And he admired that about her. He just wanted to hold her.

When they got to her car, he was surprised and chuckled.

"What's funny? Because I drive a Ford Escort? You were expecting a BMW or a Lexus?" She grinned a cheeky grin.

"Actually, no. I admire you for driving an Escort. It's compact and perfect for you. I was just thinking how ironic we parked beside each other."

"Oh," she said, chuckling. "That's your truck?"

His Ford pick-up truck was parked right beside hers. It was as if the Lord wanted them to meet that day.

"Well, I guess we have a lot in common. Parking right by the entrance."

"We sure do."

When they were close to her car, he opened the car door for her and closed it for her when she got inside. She then wound the window down.

"So, I'll meet you at the café? Or should I drive behind you?"

"No, you can go in front." He grinned.

She smiled and wound the window back down and he could feel his heart jump in his chest. This was crazy. He felt as if he'd known her forever, but right now, he wanted to spend more time with her.

When they got to the café, they found the perfect seat by the window with a gorgeous view.

They both ordered a latte and a biscuit. Perfect for an afternoon snack after church.

He noticed her eyes closed and she said a sweet grace before they ate.

"You say grace when you get coffee and biscuit?"

"For everything. My dad used to always say, be thankful for everything you get. Doesn't matter how big or small."

"I admire that about you."

"Thanks. You know the crew on the set used to make fun of me. Whenever the gofer got us coffee and a donut, I'd say grace first before I take a bite or sip. They used to think I was a strange little thing."

"They're strange for thinking that. You're being you. Nothing wrong with that."

And there was nothing wrong with that at all.

They had a wonderful time talking about all sorts of stuff. She even opened up to him about what her ex-fiancé did to her since it was all out in the open. But she wasn't bitter about it. She was happy he was happy.

She casually mentioned that she needed a date for the *Dallas Academy of Film and TV Awards* ceremony in a few weeks. She told him lightheartedly that she didn't want to show up empty handed, so to speak.

"I'd love to take you," Jesse offered, hoping he didn't sound too eager.

"Oh, no. I wasn't asking you to take me."

"I know you weren't, but I'd love to. I'd be honored to."

"You would?" She lit up.

So humble, so sweet. She didn't give off the entitled vibe. He loved that about her.

"Sure. It would be great. Besides, I'd love to meet all my favorite stars." Now, he knew she was the star he'd always had his eyes on, but he didn't want her to feel bad. Neither did he want her to feel as if he was doing her a big favor. He wanted to make sure she knew he'd really be glad to do it. Not just out of pity, either.

Right now, he thought about the strange requests in his adoptive father's will. He said he'd try the marriage of convenience thing just to fulfill his dad's last wishes, but he was falling for Bella. How long did it take to fall for someone?

He didn't know but he knew how he felt.

He breathed a sigh. Waves of anxiety washed over him and that was not like him at all. He was a cowboy who was always in control of his emotions and his feelings.

You've got one chance. Do it.

He knew that sometimes you had to take a chance and just go with it.

You've only got one life. Do it.

But what if he made a fool of himself?

What if he turned her off and she just got up and walked out of there and got a restraining order against him or something? Could he live with that? He didn't want to scare her off.

But he had to ask her.

He needed a bride. She needed a date.

Should he?

Should he ask her to marry him?

Chapter 6

Jesse was one sweet cowboy, Bella thought to herself.

He was gorgeous. He took her breath away. She'd seen many handsome men in her line of business in Hollywood, but none could come close to that stunning figure before her. That cowboy with a heart and charm that could take any girl's breath away.

And when he touched her. Oh, my goodness. Waves of pleasure rolled down her back. It was as if his energy transferred to her.

That warm southern charm and authoritative manliness turned her on. But he was warm and kind. Not boastful. And he acted like he didn't even know how gorgeous he was. Not like some of those vain co-stars she'd seen in her line of work.

All this time, she'd been visiting the Sweet Rivers Church and had heard about the Carsen brothers but never met any of them up close. She'd been acquainted with their lovely, eccentric aunt Sue Mae. Everybody knew Sue Mae and Sue Mae knew everybody.

Sue Mae made it her business to be congenial and warm and friendly to all who attended the church, even those who only came on occasion. Sue Mae was never one to bad talk anyone because they never went to church every Sunday and Bella really appreciated that.

That's why she felt safe in talking about her personal business to Sue Mae. She was a good listener and one who never shared your business with everyone. Unless, of course, it was all common knowledge stuff.

Still, Sue Mae told her that her nephew Jesse might be available to take her to the Dallas awards ceremony since she really needed a discreet date for that night. The last thing she would want would be to show up alone or with a hired date. Word would get all over town before she could say what. And she might not have much right now, but she had her pride and a girl had to hold on to what little she had.

Pride and dignity.

Those were so important to her. She knew she had to get back to work and get her life back on track and to pay off her late father's medical debts, and she knew she wasn't going to break down any doors by being labelled a reject or washed up or a has-been.

"Thank you, Jesse." Her heart filled with joy just looking into his deep beautiful eyes. There was something about him that resonated with her.

And oh, was he delicious to the eyes or what?

Talk about a hot cowboy.

He was stunning. She'd never seen such a beautiful man before. He was gorgeous. She wondered why he wasn't married already.

She'd heard about the Carsen brothers not being the marrying type. They'd all made some pact after moving back to their ranch to stay single cowboys for life, just caring for the land and livestock and their guests at the retreat lodge on their land. It was as if they had some sort of allergic reaction to marriage.

Two of them had been engaged but it never worked out, and then one of them was widowed and another was divorced. She'd heard that one of brothers had a wife who died in a tragic accident with another man in the seat beside her. It caused quite a stir. It could not have been easy for him. But she knew all too well what heartbreak felt like.

"Hey, it's no problem at all. Say, why don't you come over to the ranch later? Are you busy this afternoon? Sue Mae's making a nice dinner."

"I'd love to. Sue Mae had invited me earlier. I wasn't sure if I could make it but..." She should try to squeeze time in.

She was supposed to be rehearsing for that two-line TV commercial. Though her gut didn't feel like it, she knew she had to pay her father's medical bills and every little bit helped. She'd have to swallow her pride. It was an honest job after all, wasn't it? Money was money as long as it was clean.

She just hoped the role won't clean out her good reputation as a desirable actress.

"Well, that's settled then. I'd love to show you around the ranch."

They finished their lattes and biscuits and got up. Just then Bella froze.

"Bella, are you all right?" Jesse looked concerned.

"I..."

She could not believe it.

Her throat closed up. She could not speak.

Jesse soon followed her gaze and saw what she was looking at. A shadow of annoyance crossed his handsome face.

Chapter 7

"Who are these people?" Jesse said to a stunned-looking Bella. She looked as if she'd seen a ghost. Her beautiful complexion started to look pale. Her pretty lips parted with horror.

"P-paparazzi."

"Oh, no. Not here. Not in Sweet Rivers."

He saw a handful of men out there with cameras and zoom lenses taking snapshots of them. How long had they been there?

Jesse felt a muscle twitch in his jaw. He was half annoyed at them and half annoyed at himself for not seeing them sooner. He'd been so caught up in Bella's beautiful presence that he wasn't even focusing on what was going on around them.

He usually never let his guard down. It wasn't like him. But this was Sweet Rivers. Stuff like that didn't happen there.

Well, he wasn't about to let them get to her.

"It's okay, Bella. You'll be safe with me."

"Thanks, Jesse. I don't know what I'd do if you weren't here with me now. These guys never seem to leave me alone. Especially since..."

"I know. No need to say any more."

Jesse walked Bella out of the café as some of the customers stared in wonder and chatted amongst themselves.

Some customers pulled out their cell phones and began filming.

Wasn't there such a thing as privacy?

What ever happened to common decency around there? He sure hoped this wouldn't turn up on some social media site. For Bella's sake.

He covered her as they made their way out. Photographers started to click away with their flashing lights and cameras.

"Bella! Bella!" A few of them shouted out to her, like she was some pet. That annoyed the heck out of Jesse. A pretty lady, so kind and humble didn't deserve that kind of ambush.

A surge of emotions rushed through him with the urge to protect her at all costs.

Was anyone listening in on their conversation?

He sure hoped not. He may not have seen what was going on outside the café, but he sure knew people were minding their own business inside.

When they'd arrived earlier, he'd taken a quick glance around and made sure they had a nice cozy booth in the corner with a window.

"Bella! Bella!" Another photographer called out. *"How do you feel about John marrying Alexis?"*

Jesse tried not to curse under his breath when he heard that.

But man, that boiled his blood. What was with these people? Couldn't they leave her alone?

The shouts and the taunting from the media continued...

"Bella! Do you have any comments?"

"Bella! Are you going to the Dallas awards ceremony? John and Alexis will be there."

"Bella! John called you boring. Do you have any comments?"

"Do you have any respect?" Jesse finally answered one reporter.

"Who are you?" the reporter asked.

Jesse ignored them as Bella hid her face in his chest as they walked to their cars. He then had an idea.

He whispered to her. "Do you want me to take you to the ranch in my truck?

"Yes, please." She nodded and buried her face in his suit.

"That way they won't chase you down."

"Thank you," she said softly.

The noise from the camera flashes and clicking overwhelmed them. How could a person live like this?

He got her into his truck, closing the door behind her. He then walked over to the driver's side and got inside then started the car.

"We can come back later and get your car," he reassured her.

"Thank you, Jesse. I'm so sorry you had to see this."

"Hey, it's not your fault, okay. Don't ever take responsibility for someone else's actions."

And he meant it.

Something had to change. And now he knew what he had to do. But would she go for it?

Chapter 8

Bella was overcome with emotions.

What. Just. Happened?

Jesse just saved her from the paparazzi.

He saved her from that media ambush—from that embarrassment.

Could a girl not go for a latte in peace? All she was doing was having some downtime after church. Why on earth did they have to show up there?

When she moved back to Texas, she never thought she'd see any sign of them, especially in her hometown of Sweet Rivers. Stuff like that just didn't happen there. Everyone knew each other.

Unless...

She wondered if someone tipped the media off. Her agent was the only one who knew she was back in town and wanted to have some quiet time while she tried to figure out her next move and get her life back on track after her father's death.

What would she have done if Jesse wasn't there beside her, shielding her and carrying her away safely to his truck?

"Sorry you had to go through that," Jesse said later when they pulled up to his family's ranch.

"I'm sorry *you* had to go through that, Jesse. You only just met me."

"I feel like I've known you forever. Besides, you're practically a friend of the family. My aunt Sue Mae knows you very well and you're a member of our church."

"Well, sort of," she replied sheepishly. "Haven't been back in a while."

"That's okay. You were out of town. Then you were looking after your father. Plus you're in showbiz."

"And now you know why it's hard for me to date."

"I can only imagine."

"That's why it's common for actors to marry each other. We know the business, we understand it. It's what we signed up for. It's so hard to put any other person outside the business into the fishbowl, zoo-like living we experience. It's as if we're caged into this persona, on display for the world to watch without a shred of privacy."

There she went, going off on a rant. She'd sworn she'd not go there. But right now she was all worked up after that press intrusion. All she wanted to do was to go away and recuperate quietly. Throwing those questions in her face like that, forcing her to face the humiliation of being dumped publicly, being called boring by your ex-fiancé, *and* losing your TV show was all too much to bear.

"It must be hard with going through a break-up so publicly," Jesse said, concerned, as if reading her mind. He really knew how to pick up on what she was feeling in the moment. It was as if he was in sync with her or something.

"I can't even begin to imagine that," he continued.

"Yeah," she sighed deeply, with regret. "In this business, you've got to grow a thick layer of skin if you want to survive, not just physically but emotionally. Now you know why so many in the industry turn to the bottle. It's like we're not treated like human beings. And then we have our business displayed all over the tabloids, being ridiculed for everyone to see."

"That's horrible," he said, shaking his head. "That's just not right."

When they got out of his truck they walked for a few minutes until they arrived at their destination. Jesse then opened the door to a lovely cabin with the sign above on the door saying Cabin 3. She realized there must be about a dozen or so cabins around the area.

The land was massive. She could see miles and miles of pastures all around.

Even though she was going through turmoil right now, she couldn't help but feel so lucky and blessed to have met Jesse today. He was a warm, friendly cowboy. And a hot-looking one too. He looked pristine in his cowboy hat and suit.

He loosened his tie slightly. She realized he must be ready to wear something more comfortable and head back out on the ranch to work. She'd never really been on a ranch before but heard it's a lot of work, seven days a week.

When they walked inside the cabin, Bella's jaw fell wide open.

"It's beautiful inside," she said, gaping.

"Thanks."

"Do all the cabins on the ranch look like this?"

"Pretty much. My brothers and I occupy these cabins. Well, most of them. They come equipped with three bedrooms, a living room, den, large eat in kitchen and dining facilities, and a nice view of the pond and the ranch."

She was stunned as she glanced out the tall floor-to-ceiling windows of the log cabin. It was breathtaking.

"You must love waking up here every morning. Gosh, it's so serene here. There's a calm presence in here. I can tell you get a lot of comfort from this place."

"I do. I moved back here from New York, as did a few of my brothers when our father got too ill to look after the ranch. We all came to help out and well, we decided to stay."

He paused for a moment as if lost in thought. What was he thinking? Did he have regrets about bringing her there? Was it something else?

His gaze changed when he mentioned his father.

She'd heard they were all adopted since his father, the great and wonderful Chet Carsen was a war hero, but sustained injuries during the war and couldn't have children of his own as a result, so he adopted many of them from the foster care system and gave them a good life on the ranch and in the church. What an amazing man he was. She'd met him once a few years back when she came to visit her father after her career took off.

"You must have been so glad to make that choice. That was very noble of you."

"It's the least we could do. Family comes first. That's our motto." Again, a shadow of sadness crossed his face, then he took off his cowboy hat and placed it down.

"I wouldn't trade this life for anything right now," he said. "Ranch life is the best life."

She smiled warmly. She loved a cowboy who appreciated the finer things in life, the simpler things.

"Would you believe I never really wanted the spotlight," she said.

"You didn't?" He seemed surprised.

"No. I love the art of dramatic expression. I love theatre and acting, but showbiz is a whole different story altogether. Art is one thing. Fame is another." She shook her head, still feeling the zing of humiliation and sting of pain by that media intrusion earlier.

Media intrusion.

That was the story of her life now, wasn't it?

And the embarrassment of having that unprofessional photographer hurl those insulting questions at her while she walked with Jesse, was another layer of embarrassment she didn't think she'd be able to get over any time soon.

"I hear you," Jesse said.

She gave him an appreciative smile as he showed her around his cabin. She was glad the ranch had a gate that no one could just drive through to his front door. The dirt road was pretty much private. The guest lodge entrance was on the other side.

She was safe. For now.

Truth be told, she really didn't want to go back out there right now to face them. It was hard enough going through her own emotional turmoil over losing her beloved father and her fiancé and her job all in the space of a month.

She needed time to hide away and get herself together. To debrief. To grieve properly. To regain her strength and to focus. But she sure could not do it with aggressive media personnel shoving their zoom-length cameras in her face, clicking away and then uploading all sorts of crazy things about her for the world to see. That was the last thing she needed.

But right now, she had a nice caring cowboy in her corner, and that made her heart melt with gratitude.

The last thing she wanted to do was to be a burden to him.

Jesse had agreed to take her to the Dallas awards ceremony. He probably didn't know he'd be signing up for this too.

Later, Jesse made scrumptious dinner for Bella of tasty chicken-fried steak and creamy mashed potatoes. He also served some of Sue Mae's famous Southern Sweet Tea.

There was something appealing about a handsome, strong cowboy who also knew his way around a kitchen. Bella loved that about him.

After she helped him wash and dry the dishes, they stood in the kitchen talking.

"We usually have dinner together at the main house on Sundays," Jesse said, "but you said you just wanted to be alone, so I told Sue Mae, I'd be making something for you."

"Thanks, Jesse, I really appreciate all you've done, but I feel so bad about putting you out..."

"Hey, you're not putting me out. It's a pleasure to be in your company. What's more important right now is that you're okay. You've been through a lot, losing your father and everything all at the same time."

She appreciated that he didn't throw the whole fiancé-dumping incident in her face and talk about her losing her TV show too. She appreciated his tactfulness in his words. It hurt to hear it out loud that her future plans of being a bride were in shambles and her career possibly over. It was overwhelming to say the least.

"You know you can stay here as long as you like, Bella. I have a spare room upstairs down the hall or one downstairs here on the main floor. Just say the word. And don't worry, I'll be out of your way."

Out of her way?

She didn't want him out of her way, not one bit. She wanted him there beside her. She didn't want to be alone right now. She couldn't take it. She felt so alone now and needed someone by her side.

She wondered if the good Lord had them cross paths today for a reason.

Her heart was overcome with warmth and appreciation for Jesse.

"You mean I can stay here? Are you sure?"

"Yes, I'm sure."

"Thank you, Jesse. It means a lot to me. I didn't know we'd be hit with a firestorm of media intrusion earlier."

"Hey, it's not your fault," he said again, his tone so warm and reassuring. Tingles of delight swirled through her body.

Gosh, he was so gentle and caring.

"I know, but...I appreciate it all the same. I'm sure you had other plans today..."

"For the Lord to use me as He sees fit. And that's what I'm doing here now, I guess." He grinned and his smile touched her heart.

She didn't want to cry right now, but she was getting emotional inside.

"Can I hug you," she said, softly. "I don't usually ask for hugs by the way. But...well...hugs are good therapy, you know. It releases that feel-good feeling of security hormone from the brain," she babbled on.

She could use a hug right now and she hoped she didn't seem to forward about it. But she felt as if she'd fall apart right now. Everything was hitting her at the same time. Coming from all directions.

Before she could say anything else, Jesse reached down and gave her a good bear hug. She felt his warmth and energy and the scent of his cologne wafted to her nose and she felt an overwhelming attraction to him.

Was this kismet?

She'd never felt this way about her ex-fiancé. Nothing like that at all. She never knew she could feel this way. There was something about Jesse that just connected to her soul. She felt that instant chemistry when they'd met after service. It was a palpable feeling of trust, attraction. She didn't know how else to describe it.

They pulled away after a nice long hug. Her breath caught in her throat. She could sense he felt something too.

"I....uh...I hope I wasn't out of line asking you for a hug just now."

"Out of line? Of course not, Bella."

Was he flushing? Was that a hint of rouge in his cheeks?

"I wish there was something I could do for you, Jesse. Anything. You have no idea how you saved me just now."

"Think nothing of it."

"Listen, I...I'd better make a call. I'll need to have my assistant bring my things over. Thank you for offering to take me in so I'll have a roof over my head with a little privacy."

"Like I said, I don't mind one bit. Stay as long as you like," he reiterated.

He then paused for a moment as if in thought.

"What's wrong?"

"You know folks will start to talk about you being here. I just don't want you to have to go through another round of gossip."

"I know," she said, biting down on her lower lip.

"I may have a solution."

"You do?"

"Yes. You said you wished you could do something for me in return. Well, first of all, I'm not a tit for tat kind of guy. When I do something, it's with my right hand. I don't expect anything back."

"But...?"

He grinned. "Well, this is sort of different. I was looking for something...or *someone* for a favor..."

"Hey, count me in. Looks like we're in this together now. Besides, they already have you connected to me."

"So why not make it legit?"

"Legit? Now, just what are you getting at, cowboy?" she grinned, playfully, arching her brow. She was enjoying his company and anything that took her mind away from her troubles.

She'd do anything for Jesse. Anything at all.

"Will you marry me?"

Chapter 9

Jesse thought he'd made a huge mistake asking Bella to marry him like that. What was he thinking? Maybe he needed to explain more.

"What did you just say?" Bella's pretty eyes widened in surprise.

"Oh, no. Not that way. I mean just as a pretence."

She laughed nervously. "Oh, you had me for a minute. I thought you were really serious."

"Actually…" He hesitated for a moment, not sure of how much to tell her right now. But oh, her laugh was contagious.

He grinned to himself. Despite what she was going through, he felt a light energy around her, a jovial spirit.

"Oh, you mean so that the media doesn't think I'm just shacking up with someone? Good. I like that," she said, thoughtfully. She chuckled. "Actually, I like that a lot."

She was a fighter, he knew that and felt that. She was someone who refused to let the world dim her spirit. He admired that about her. She was a matter-of-fact girl, who just got things done. He didn't know why, but he just picked up on that about her.

"Sort of. You're in the middle of an image crisis and if anyone asks, you could just say that we're together."

"Actually," she turned around and thought for a moment. Then she turned to face him, her face lit up. "Could you pretend to be my uh…my fiancé."

"Your fiancé? You want me to pretend to be your fiancé?" Was he hearing things? His heart leaped for joy in his chest.

Here was the one woman he'd been secretly admiring for so many years and now she wasn't on the TV, but in his own home and now in his heart and she wanted him to pretend to be her fiancé?

"I'm sorry if that's too forward it's just that, as you say this is an image crisis and I need to get things together before I make my first public appearance. My ex made it sound like..."

"You don't need to explain any further." His blood boiled up just thinking about what that guy did, even if he was drunk in a bar at the time when he was being secretly recorded on someone's phone, John should have been more careful. Tarnishing the reputation of such a fine actress and perfect lady was all wrong.

"This is crazy, isn't it?" she said.

"Not really, if you think about it. Life is like one big adventure. You never know what you'll come up against, but sometimes you just have to go with the flow, have a bit of fun and improvise. Or else it would be just boring, wouldn't it?"

He'd always played it safe, trying to keep his distance because he didn't want to get hurt as he'd been in the past. But this was different, wasn't it? This was Bella Lovely; someone he practically knew very well. She wasn't just some stranger on the street. She was a member of his church and a friend of the family.

He'd be more than honored to do this for her. And who knew, it could turn into so much more.

He thought for a moment. She obviously thought he was joking before when he'd asked her to marry him as a pretence. Maybe he needed to explain further.

"I don't know if Sue Mae told you this, but my late father made a stipulation in his will."

"A stipulation?" she asked, concerned.

"Yes. Since we can talk straight with each other and well, we can trust each other, right?"

"Right. Of course. I know you would never go to anyone and tell them what we've just discussed."

"Of course not. Well," he said, pacing. "My father had made it clear that before complete ownership of the ranch is shared amongst us, we need to be married."

"What? So you were serious before when you asked me to marry you?"

"Well, yes and no. I mean, it wouldn't have to be real. We'd just pretend to be married. I mean, we'd get married but it wouldn't be a real marriage. Just in name only."

"Wow!" She sat down for a moment, soaking it all in.

He guessed this really caught her off guard.

Then...

She chuckled.

Then she burst out into a full-blown laughter. It was a beautiful hearty laugh. He fell in love with the sound coming from her lips as she shook with laughter. It was good seeing her happy for once, since she'd been very serious since the breakup of her ex and the death of her father.

"What's so funny?" he finally asked.

"Oh, it's not what you think. I'm not laughing at you. I'm laughing at us."

"You're laughing at *us*? I don't get it."

"Well, aren't we a pair. I think the Lord brought us together for a reason."

"Now, I don't doubt that for a moment."

"You know something, I need a fake fiancé, you need a fake bride. I say let's do it!"

"You sure about that now?"

"Yes, I'm sure." She drew in a deep breath. "But first, I need to know a little bit more, such as how long we're supposed to *pretend* to be married?"

"Well, here's the thing. We need to really get married, live here for a while. Maybe for six months or a year, then once the lawyer sees the certificate and sees that we're married and transfers land ownership to all our names..." He swallowed hard, not wanting to say the next part. "We could go our separate ways..."

He said it but something deep down inside him didn't mean the last part. In fact, he'd finally found someone he thought he could stay with.

Their spirits just seem to connect with each other, and he hadn't even been around her long, though he'd known her for many years.

Just then her cell phone rang. She looked at the screen.

"Is it the press?"

"No, it's my agent," she said. "I should take this call."

"You want some privacy?"

"Oh, no. Please stay. You're my fiancé, after all." She grinned.

A lightness came around his heart.

She answered the call.

Then another thought struck him. Was Bella going to tell her agent their little secret?

Chapter 10

"Moss, so glad you called." Bella smiled into the phone.

"So glad I called? Are you kidding me? Lady, you're all over the internet right now."

"What?" Her heart sank. "All over the Internet? Are you sure?" Bella hadn't checked her web browser or her social media feeds yet.

Boy, those paparazzi sure work fast.

"Yeah, you and this cowboy. I couldn't see his face in the picture because of his hat. His face was obscured. But he is tall, isn't he?"

"Yes, he is."

"He was shielding you from the paps. What is he? A bodyguard? You hired a bodyguard and didn't tell me? Am I going to be receiving a bill for this?"

"Moss, calm down. I didn't hire a bodyguard."

Though it felt as if Jesse was her protector and so much more. Funny, how they'd only been acquainted for such a short time and yet she felt as if she'd known him forever. She'd only known about him, but never had the chance to meet him in person until today. And what a time to meet him—in the middle of a huge public scandal.

"He's uh..." She looked over at Jesse. He gave her an encouraging look.

"He's my uh...my date."

"Your date? So you're dating someone now and you forgot to tell me?"

"Moss, it's not like that. I've known his family forever. We go to the same church. We met up in church."

"Whoa! This is great!" Moss said to Bella over the phone, his voice now filled with excitement. "Boy, things work fast down at your church."

"What are you talking about, Moss?" She felt the sting of insult just now. Did her agent think she planned this?

"You know what I mean," Moss said. "You said you were going to pray on it, on your situation, remember?"

"Yes, but you made it sound like..."

"Oh, never mind, Bella. I'm just glad you found someone. Will he be attending the *Dallas Academy of Film and TV Awards* ceremony with you? Please tell me he'll be attending the awards ceremony with you."

"Yes, Moss, he says he can make it."

Bella explained to Moss what was going on but saw the look of horror on Jesse's face.

Maybe she should have explained to Jesse that her agent could be trusted.

Well, she left out the part about Jesse's own reason for getting hitched when speaking with Moss, of course. That was Jesse's private business. But her agent already knew *her* dilemma and wanted to help her with her image.

"Good. Uh..." Moss hesitated for a moment. That wasn't like him.

"Moss, you still there?" she said into the phone, while Jesse left the living room area and went into the kitchen to give them a bit of space. Not that she minded him being there.

"Is he uh...you know..."

"Is he what, Moss?" Her voice was more stern now. She could only guess what Moss was getting at.

"You know. Is he red-carpet friendly?"

"Red-carpet friendly?" Bella was stunned. "Now, I know I've heard it all."

"Well, *is* he? You know it helps your image if you're with a hot-looking guy. Not anyone too homely."

"Moss!"

"Hey, listen. I don't make the rules. That's just how it is in this business. You know that."

Yeah, and she was beginning to rethink whether or not she really wanted to *stay* in this business.

But it's just that her heart and soul belonged to the world of dramatic arts. There was no other thing she wanted to do but act. And right now, she had the chance of the role of her life in that new rom-com. That would be just what she needed to get her life back on track. To pay off her father's medical debts and to feel like a person again.

"Yes, he's all that and more. He's a good-looking cowboy with a heart of gold."

And she meant it. She meant every single word of it. And her heart jolted with agreement. There was something about Jesse that really touched her soul. Not to mention he was pleasing to the eyes, a gorgeous cowboy with all the right features, handsome face, tall, muscular body, strength in body and in personality and character. What more could she ask for?

Part of her wished they were really a couple. But she knew that relationships, real relationships, were way too risky. She wasn't going to go down *that* road again. After what her ex did to her heart, she just couldn't open her soul to that much vulnerability again. Still, this was fun, wasn't it?

It was a nice escape from her troubles. A fake relationship to keep the media vultures and the relationship critics off her back so she could focus on getting her career back on track and spreading joy to others through her art. Her acting.

She could see from the corner of her eyes, that Jesse grinned and shook his head. She was glad she got that reaction from him. The last thing she would want was to insult him in any way. He was more than just a new friend. He was a hero in the moment, saving her from despair and humiliation.

What a cowboy.

"Well, I'm glad you and your good-looking cowboy are hitting it off. So what do you want me to say? My phone has been ringing off the hook with the press wanting to know what's going on. What should I tell them?"

"You can tell them...tell them nothing."

"Now you know they might keep digging if we don't give them something."

"They might go digging further if we do."

"Okay, you've got a point. But we need to tell them something. I mean, they saw you go into that nice ranch there with the cowboy. I'm sure they'll be staking outside the gates waiting for you to reappear."

Moss had a good point. She didn't like the way the press behaved, and feeding them might have them coming back for more.

"You know it's been a little while since your father died and since John broke off with you. It wouldn't be too much off the mark for you to have found someone else. Let them know you've moved on and they can leave you alone and whatever John said about you not being desirable or being too boring won't hold water. Besides, remember, James' new rom-com still doesn't have a lead."

Her heart jumped inside her just thinking about it. She knew that role was meant for her. Olson James was a winner when it came to his rom coms. They always broke box office records. She always wanted to work with that Hollywood producer and director. And to think he would be in Dallas soon for the Dallas awards show. He was top of the game. It would help her out of her depressive state to work on a romantic comedy. She bit down on her lower lip as she thought about it for a moment. She sighed deeply.

"Give me a moment, Moss." She turned the phone on mute.

"Jesse," she said. "Do you mind if Moss tells the press that I'm engaged." She looked at him squeamishly hoping he wouldn't say he minded.

He thought about it for a moment.

Her heart pounded in her chest.

This meant the world to her. Moss was right. Since Jesse was going to be her date for the awards ceremony and they'd be in a fake relationship, it was probably wise to set the record straight from now so there would be no false rumors flying around.

She had to control the narrative from now on, before the media made up its own story. But would Jesse go for it? This would thrust him into the spotlight big time once they started digging up whatever they could find on her new fiancé.

All of a sudden, she didn't want to do this. She didn't want Jesse to have to go through this. This was *her* problem, not his.

But then again, he needed a bride to convince the lawyers he was serious about marriage too, didn't he?

Still, going public with an actress embroiled in a publicity scandal since last year probably wasn't what this cowboy signed up for.

What was he going to say?

Chapter 11

"You did what?" Chase said to Jesse on Monday morning after they'd just finished feeding the cows. They both took off their cowboy hats and took a break by the side at the west fence, the sunrise peeked over the horizon, creating a warm morning glow on the ranch.

Earlier, he had made breakfast for Bella and left it on the stove for her with a note. He sure hoped she liked what he made for her. He wanted her to feel as comfortable as possible. He left her there in her own room, sleeping like an angel. When he'd knocked on the door and peeked inside to let her know he'd be heading out, she was sound asleep.

And man, did she look beautiful even in her sleep. Like a sleeping beauty.

"I agreed to be her fiancé for the Dallas Academy of Film awards ceremony. And she...agreed to enter a marriage of convenience for a short period of time. A win-win situation."

Chase looked stunned.

"How on earth did you get Bella Lovely to agree to marry you? She's...she's a star."

"Yeah, thanks for your vote of confidence, bro."

"Oh, no. You know I didn't mean it that way, Jesse. You need to be careful with her."

"What's that supposed to mean?"

"It's one thing to ask an ordinary girl to marry you, but Bella Lovely is tabloid material. She has a whole lot of baggage she's carrying around. She's everywhere on the internet these days. Have you thought about your privacy? What if she blows this whole thing over? The lawyer won't be impressed if he thought we were just faking marriage to get ownership of the ranch."

"Relax, bro. It's not like that. She's discreet. She's got just as much at stake as we do here."

"Okay, bro. I just don't want to see you get hurt. She's lovely and all, and pun intended, but just be careful. The media can chew you up and spit you out without a second thought if you're not careful. Once you get on their radar, that's it. They might go digging up stuff about you."

"I don't believe that for one second. Besides, they won't find much. You know I keep to myself."

"I know. And that's what worries me. I know you like her, Jesse. You've been watching her on TV for years but being a part of her world might force you into the public eye."

"I thought about it, Chase. I care a lot about her. She's all heart and soul. She gave up her career to care for her dying father and now she's left with all his medical bills. She needs to get her life back on track. She's not what you think. She's really a shy down-to-earth girl. She just happens to be one heck of an actress and loves acting."

"Yeah, that's the problem."

"What's the problem."

"The acting part, bro. She's an actress."

Jesse didn't like that tone one bit, though deep down he knew his brother loved him and was just looking out for him, but he also knew what he felt inside.

Jesse felt this was the right thing to do. Right now, he couldn't think of anyone else he'd rather marry. Even if it was for a short time.

This was the right thing to do, wasn't it?

Chapter 12

Bella's heart filled with joy when she saw the lovely note on the table and the hot breakfast on the stove. Did Jesse really do that for her?

She was used to doing sentimental stuff like that for everyone else, but no one had ever done that for her before. No one.

The coffee was already freshly brewed and tasted delicious to her lips. But it was his scrambled eggs and fluffy pancakes with fresh blueberries on the side that really did it for her.

How on earth did he learn to cook breakfast like that?

There wasn't anything that handsome cowboy couldn't do. She felt so blessed to have crossed his path at the right time in her life. She was so grateful for him.

Her stomach tightened into knots thinking of what she would be putting him through with all this publicity. She only hoped the press would be gentle with him. He wasn't a cowboy that got around anyway. He stayed mostly on the ranch, went into town to get supplies, and attended the local church. It wasn't exactly tabloid-material.

They'd spent hours talking last night getting to know more about each other. He was a guy who one would call deep in his philosophies about life.

His adoptive father certainly rubbed off on him in a positive way. She could not imagine what it would be like to be adopted and what Jesse went through when his biological family could no longer care for him. She didn't blame him one bit for keeping his heart guarded as much as he did.

She wished she could have seen him this morning before he left. That was her regret right now. She at least wanted to thank him for the lovely breakfast and for everything he was doing for her. She only wished she could do more for him. This marriage of convenience thing would help him keep ownership of the ranch and she was all too happy to go through with it.

Just then her cell phone buzzed and she remembered to turn on the ringer. She often turned it off at night before she went to bed so she could get a good night's sleep and not have to be woken up in the night. The only time she had kept her phone on during the night was when her father took ill. She wanted to be accessible to him day and night. But when he passed away, a huge part of her went with him. She started losing sleep and it was getting the better of her nerves. Her doc had told her to prioritize getting sleep. He gave her some over-the-counter sleep hormone to help her out and helped her to restructure her habits, so no more staying up late at night.

Her heart leapt in her chest thinking it could be Jesse calling.

She frowned when she saw it wasn't him. It was Lizzy, one of her co-stars from her now defunct TV show calling. Lizzy and Bella had become friends over the years though Lizzy was now busy working on another set and didn't have much time to socialize as she did before with her hectic filming schedule.

Bella was truly happy Lizzy landed another part right after their show had been cancelled. She deserved it. She worked so hard as an actress. It wasn't easy with her dyslexia. Bella would often help her friend when reading scripts and Lizzy had always appreciated that.

"Hey Lizzy. Good morning," Bella said as cheerfully as she could, feeling guilty because she wished it had been Jesse on the other end of the phone.

"Bella, good morning to you too." Lizzy's voice sounded so excited. Bella could only guess why.

"You sound cheerful."

"I heard the good news," Lizzy said. "Congratulations!"

Word certainly travelled fast. Gossip was the only thing that traveled quicker than email or text.

"Don't tell me, you saw it online somewhere?" Bella said with a grin.

"Yes, yes, yes. Why didn't you tell me, girl? I am so happy for you! Congratulations!"

Bella felt Lizzy's genuine enthusiasm and it warmed her soul. If only her relationship with Jesse were real.

Of course, no one could know that part. Except her agent, of course, since it was his idea to help her repair her fractured image in the public eye. It would also be good for his agency too, if she got more work. He certainly worked hard for his fifteen percent commission off any work she did.

"Thanks, Lizzy, that's so sweet of you."

"Did you set the date yet? Have you chosen a maid of honor?" Her excitement was contagious and for a fleeting moment Bella felt it in her very soul.

But then that feeling evaporated with the reality that it was only a fake engagement. But if she had to be honest with herself, as much as she vowed to never get close to anyone again or to never marry, it felt good being with Jesse. He made her feel so wonderful.

In fact, she'd felt more amazing in the last twenty-four hours in his presence than she'd felt in the two years she'd been engaged to John. Imagine that? Well, what did that say about her previous relationship?

She'd always heard about this kismet thing and that everyone had a soul mate.

In fact, her father told her that when she met the right one, she'd know. And it wouldn't take forever to find out. But the trouble was, this new relationship wasn't real, was it?

But then why did her feelings for Jesse feel so real?

"No, I haven't chosen a date yet or a maid of honor." Bella smiled into the phone. "But you know, I would be honored if you have time..."

Before she could finish, Lizzy squealed into the phone. "Of course! I'd love to be your maid of honor!"

Bella felt warmth come over her.

"Thank you, Lizzy." She also knew this would be good for Jesse. Having a well-known actress as a maid of honor to his new bride would make a convincing case for his marriage agreement.

Later, Bella got ready in her room. She'd just had the most amazing shower. She couldn't believe how neat Jesse kept his place, including his bathroom. It was so welcoming walking into a nice guest room down the hall with fresh linen and a perfect view of the ranch estate. The sunrise glowed into her room, so she was facing the east. She loved that. No wonder she woke up with a lot more energy this morning.

She took out a few dresses and wasn't sure which one to wear.

She held the red one up to her and looked in the full-length mirror in the room. She then scrunched up her nose. What was with her? She must have gone through a dozen outfits. Then she realized she was on a ranch now. She needed to be casual, but nice casual.

Last night, her assistant had brought over her suitcase with most of her stuff. She didn't want to go back to the apartment right now to face any intruding visitors lurking outside and was glad she had accepted the help from her agent, Moss. The assistant worked for him but often did errands for his top clients too.

Bella could not have afforded to hire her personally right now if it wasn't for her agent. They didn't always see eye to eye on different assignments, but she was glad for Moss. She knew he looked out for her and she appreciated it.

Bella decided to wear a nice pair of blue hip-hugging jeans with a bit of Lycra material in it for comfort. Then she donned a nice shirt that was comfortable and attractive at the same time. Okay, so what if she was in a fake relationship? She still wanted to look her best for her handsome cowboy fiancé, didn't she?

She sighed deeply. Having gotten ready, she took a quick peek in the closet and looked at her ensembles. She would need to head into town soon to get a nice dress for the awards show. That was a must. She wondered if Jesse had a nice tux for the occasion. She assumed he would, but then again, he spent most of his time on the ranch. He had some nice suits for church, but he would need a fancy tux for the *Dallas Academy of Film* awards ceremony. A red-carpet-style tux. That was not going to be cheap, but she'd see what could be done. The last thing she would want would be for him to be out of pocket for this gig. It was *her* idea, after all.

She would need to find a dress for the awards show and a dress for her engagement and her wedding. All of a sudden, she just realized her budget was going to go through the roof.

Later, at noon time, Bella decided to make a nice lunch for Jesse. She still hadn't heard anything from him. And the view from the windows in the cabin didn't show the full ranch, only a part of it. She saw a few horses out there and some cows grazing in another arena.

Her heart pounded with anxiety now. Was Jesse having second thoughts?

She sure hoped not. Was he keeping his distance from her because he wondered what the heck he'd gotten into?

Stop being dramatic, Bella. He's a busy cowboy, remember? There's a lot of work to do on the ranch.

She tried to console herself.

That was the trouble with having a lot of time on your hands, your mind tended to work overtime. Her imagination could get a bit crazy at times.

Having been through the relationship ringer and having her ex-fiancé do a number on her heart, made her doubt herself at times. Wondering if she just had some sort of invisible repellent where men were concerned. Did they spot her a mile off and realize they didn't want to be around her?

Stop that, Bella. Positive thoughts. Only think positive thoughts.

The truth was, she'd been so busy and caught up with being there for her father during his illness that she hadn't spent much time at all with John. But you'd think John would've understood her situation. Her father was terminally ill. There was no way she had any emotional energy left for her fiancé at that time. But then maybe it was something else. Maybe she just didn't want to be too close to anyone because she kept losing those close to her. Her mother died at her birth, she'd lost her grandmother and her grandfather and now her father.

Maybe it was psychological. She kept her distance from others because it was safer.

Was that what drove John away and into the arms of another woman?

She tried not to blame herself but wondered if she should shoulder the blame. But then again, Lizzy had told her it wasn't her fault. John was just a flirting type of guy and he wasn't all that he was cracked up to be. But maybe her friend was just being kind.

Just then she heard the sound of the keys dangling as the front door opened and her heart leaped with excitement. She heard whistling coming from downstairs. Why did she feel as if she were in a real relationship? She suddenly felt like the doting 1950s wife beaming with joy as her husband walked through the door. Now all she would need would be two point four children and a family dog.

She grinned to herself at the thought.

"Honey, I'm home," Jesse's strong and sexy voice came from downstairs.

Bella smiled to herself and made her way down the steps. She didn't know what got into her just now, but all of a sudden, she saw herself in a role. The role of loving fiancée.

That's what helped her through life and got her through the tough times. If she acted a part long enough, she'd convince yourself that she was really that person.

That, of course, could be a double-edged sword if you got too connected to a character only to have your show cancelled.

"Well, hello darling. And how was your day today?" Bella said playfully to her handsome cowboy fiancé, putting her arms around the top of his shoulders.

She knew it was only noon. But they could play this couple, couldn't they? Life was too short to be too serious.

Play a little. Live a little That's what her dear late father used to say. And he made sure they lived a good life. Lots of laughter and light-heartedness every day, no matter what was going on in their life.

"It's even better now that you're here," he said with his sweet southern charm.

A smile wide as the ocean crossed his handsome face as he held her.

When he touched her back, she felt his warm energy transfer through her, butterflies tickled her tummy.

There was something magical about his touch. She looked into his beautiful brown eyes, admiring his gorgeous bone structure and those lovely thick long lashes. Why was it that handsome men had all the long lashes?

"Well, now that's a lovely thought. Same here," she replied.

For a moment, her heart hammered hard in her chest.

Was he going to kiss her?

Their lips were so close, the scent of his sexy cologne wafted to her nose. His touch sent her pulse racing as a quiver surged through her veins.

Kiss me, she wanted to say. But she couldn't. They were only a pretend couple.

Still, the magnetic pull was there. It was undeniable. He then lowered his head down to hers and...

The sound of someone clearing their throat distracted them. It was Sue Mae at the door. When Jesse walked in, he'd forgotten to close the door behind him.

"Sue Mae. Nice to see you. Come in," Jesse said, pulling away from Bella. She could see a hint of rouge coloring his cheeks.

"Nice to see you too, Jesse. Bella," Sue Mae nodded to Bella also. "I just brought over some strawberries. I thought you might like some. Freshly picked."

"Thanks Sue Mae."

"Well, aren't you two the loving couple," Sue Mae added as she placed the basket on the table. "I didn't mean to interrupt what you two were doing."

"Oh, no. We were just..." *Just what? Playing?*

They were having a bit of fun with each other. It was like they could read each other's minds and they just clicked. But they had no idea there was a witness behind them at the time. Still, Bella felt her pulses race when she embraced him, and he held her back. It was surreal.

"Well, I knew I was right." Sue Mae beamed proudly at Jesse and Bella.

Both Bella and Jesse exchanged funny glances and looked puzzled at Sue Mae.

"You knew you were right?" Jesse asked, confused.

"Yes, you know. About my instincts. I knew you two would hit it off right away and make a great match. Didn't take long though, did it? I must admit this will be my all-time record. Twenty-four hours and you two are already engaged. I know they work really fast in Hollywood, but here in Texas?" Sue Mae grinned. "This is one for the Guinness Book of World Records."

"Sue Mae, it's not exactly like that. We're going to take our time to get to know each other first. Jesse was so kind to agree to come with me to the awards show."

"Hmm-mmm." Sue Mae smiled.

"I'm sure it's not the shortest engagement," Jesse said.

"Well, it's not the longest," Sue Mae added. "I really want you two to be happy. You should see what they're saying about you two online."

"What are they saying?" Jesse asked, curious.

"Oh, no. I don't want to know," Bella added.

"And why not?" Sue Mae asked.

"My dad always said it's not healthy to read stuff about yourself, especially online. That's not good for your mental health. Everyone has an opinion. I don't want to invite their thoughts into my head."

"Atta girl," Jesse said. "She's right, Sue Mae. We don't need to know what they're saying about us online. The only opinions that count are from those close to us and our own."

"You're right, my dear nephew. But it's still good to know about the positive things. That can't hurt."

"Again, I don't want to get too caught up in what others think of me." Bella stood by her words.

"You're not the least bit curious?" Sue Mae said.

"Yes and no," Bella said. "If there's anything defamatory or anything that I should know about my agent or my legal team handles that. Otherwise, I try not to get too sucked into all that."

"Well, you are wise. You sound like your father. He was always thinking about ways to keep your spirit up and to focus on the positive sides of life."

"I know," Bella said, quietly. She missed her father dearly. Her heart squeezed thinking about him and how much she wished he could have been around longer. But she knew he was with the Lord now and that gave her comfort that he was no longer suffering. He was at peace.

"Well, don't worry about what they said about your engagement," Sue Mae said.

Bella wanted to ask what they were talking about. But she decided not to. If it was anything dangerous or anything she should respond to, her agent, Moss, would let her know. Or he'd handle it himself.

"You know the longest engagement on record was between a man named Octavio Guillan and Adriana Martinez. They finally got married after 67 years in June 1969. Can you believe it?" Sue Mae said.

"A sixty-seven-year engagement?"

"Yes."

"Where? Here in Texas?"

"Oh, no. In Mexico City. They got married at 82. Please don't wait that long. Besides, Jesse, you know you shouldn't wait that long." Sue Mae grinned.

"I know, Sue Mae. I know."

"And what's the shortest engagement on record?" Bella asked, curious.

"I believe that would be you two." Sue Mae winked.

Chapter 13

"Would you like to stay for lunch? I made some hamburgers," Bella offered Sue Mae.

"I'd love to, but I must run now. I'll leave you two alone." She smiled and gave Jesse a peck on the cheek. She winked to them and left.

Jesse grinned, shaking his head.

"Sorry about that," he said to Bella.

"Sorry about what? Your aunt is lovely. She always is."

"I forgot you know her well."

"Very well from our ladies' meeting at the church, whenever I am in town, of course."

Later, they sat down to eat lunch. He wasn't expecting her to make him anything. Heck, he'd planned to pamper her this whole time. He knew Bella had been so busy caring for her ailing father during the last months of her father's life, she'd been up all night every night with her dad, tending to his needs, day and night.

Jesse wanted to be the one to take care of Bella, for a change, while she was with him. Give her a break. He was well aware of caregiver burnout and knew it couldn't have been easy for her, especially since she had no other close family members.

Yep, he knew a lot about her life, from what he'd read about her in the TV Guide and online and from what she'd told him last night.

Jesse couldn't help but think he'd almost kissed Bella.

Just thinking about it sent his heartbeat racing over the speed limit. He could feel that sweet magnetic pull between them. They really had hot chemistry. He could not deny it. She was a stunning beauty, even without her set makeup.

"You know, I can't thank you again for what you're doing for me, Jesse," she said, gently after they finished their lunch.

Right now, he wished he could just reach across the table and hug her and hold her in his arms, pressing his lips to hers. She looked so breathtaking.

"Hey, like I said, it's my pleasure. And I can't thank you enough for what you're going to do for me too."

"It's funny how things work out. We both need to be married or settled down for a reason—other than love." Her voice trailed off at the end.

He wished he could tell her that once they were married and living under the same roof, it wouldn't matter. Just like his brothers Beau and Luke, closeness might bring them together. They may end up falling in love. The thought sent his pulse pounding with delight.

"Love is so overrated, isn't it?" she said.

"What do you mean?"

"Well, so much emphasis is placed on marriage for love. As Sue Mae said people get married for all kinds of reasons. We shouldn't feel weird about our upcoming wedding."

"You're right," he agreed.

"And speaking of which, I thought about our wedding day. What do you think about us both being in white?"

"I think that would be fine."

She smiled. "I'm glad you said that. I'm going to ask my agent to see if he can get us a deal on a white tux from the designer...."

"Whoa, wait a minute now. No need for that."

"What do you mean?"

"I don't mean it like that. I mean I can afford to get my own tux. We're doing pretty well out here. I might live the simple life, but we're not hurting for cash down here."

She smiled. "I'm sorry, I didn't mean to..."

"No worries. No need to explain. And I didn't mean to come across that way either."

She got up and walked over to his side. He rose from the table. She snaked her arms around him and he embraced her too.

The surge of heat that raced inside him made him want to kiss her.

Instead, he just stroked her hair. It was as if they had some sort of understanding. They didn't need to say much. They just knew what each other felt.

He never thought he'd meet a woman that had such an understanding like that with him. After snapping at her like that earlier, most women would have just walked but she knew he didn't mean it.

He felt that she knew he had his pride and just wanted to make sure that he was not misunderstood.

He couldn't wait for them to get married and live under the same roof. Even if it were just for a year or six months.

"So how long do you want to stay here after we get married?" he asked her, hoping she'd say forever.

"I guess a year should be good."

He wanted to shout for joy. It was better than six months. Wow! A year living with Bella Lovely as his wife? He couldn't be happier.

"If you don't mind," she added.

"That's sweet. That's fine by me." He was glad he was still holding her and she couldn't see the wide smile on his face.

"That should keep the lawyer off my back since I'd fulfill my obligation as per father's will."

"Good. Looks like we'll both have what we need."

"Yes, we will." He then pulled back and looked deep into her beautiful eyes.

But then he saw something in them that he hadn't seen before. Was that doubt?

Chapter 14

The following week, Bella finished reading a few scripts that her agent sent her while sitting in her guest room at Jesse's cabin.

The scripts were only a few lines for each role. She wasn't happy with this selection, but she'd have to take whatever work she could get. How on earth did a TV sitcom actress come to this?

She knew very well. One of the directors from her past once told her he'd give her a part if she dated him, but she gave him a big fat "no."

After that, she never heard back from him. But that was all good, because she didn't want a role that way. She wanted to get it by working hard, not by who she dated. That's why she really wanted to work with Olson James. He had such a good reputation in the industry and all his movies were hits.

"Sorry, Bella," Moss had told her over the phone earlier. "James still hasn't made a decision yet."

She'd auditioned for Olson James two days ago. She left town discreetly with a limo that the agent sent for her to pick her up from the ranch. James was in Texas at the time and was available to hold auditions in Dallas at a hotel, so it wasn't a long drive from Sweet Rivers.

James seemed to like her audition, but he didn't give her an answer at the time. She couldn't help but wonder if it had anything to do with the media frenzy and the fact that her once eligible bachelor fiancé is now getting married to an A-list actress after calling her too boring to be around.

That really crushed her pride at the time. She had to fight back. And she knew just how she was going to do it.

"Well, let me know as soon as he does make a decision," she'd told Moss.

"I will, you know that. Besides, I've got my own bills to pay around here," he chuckled. "Speaking of which, how's life on the ranch?"

She didn't know how bills and ranch were related but...

"It's been a week and it's been lovely, enjoying the sunsets on the ranch, watching the cows graze, and the beautiful horses, the simple life, nature...I love it all. Thanks for asking."

But she wanted to do so much more. She wanted to spend time with Jesse on the ranch, but that cowboy always seemed so busy. She hadn't realized how much work and upkeep the ranch took. The last thing she would want to do was get in his way, but she really wanted more time with him. She loved the way she felt around him. His positive energy, his wit, his charm...and oh, that tall frame of his and his wonderful physique.

"Nice. Well, I'm glad you're having a relaxing time out there. But you two haven't been seen together since that week."

"And that's for the best."

"There's still a lot of buzz going on about you getting your life back together with this new man."

"I know."

"Well, it should be fun. At least people will know once they see you two looking lovely on the red carpet next week."

Her nerves were a jangle thinking about it. It would be her first public appearance since her big public break up with John and the death of her father. But she could handle it. She knew she had no choice but to move forward.

Later, when she heard Jesse come in through the front door, she finally mustered the courage to ask Jesse something she'd been dying to ask him all week.

She picked up the nerve to finally talk to Jesse, who had just finished helping his brother fix a post on the west fence.

He got back inside the cabin and he took off his cowboy hat.

"So, how was your day, cowboy?" she asked cheerfully.

She couldn't help but notice the grin that curved his sweet lips.

"Nice, now that you're in front of me."

She loved that flirting between them. She wished it could last forever, but she knew that it was only for a short time.

"Good. You know I was just wondering..."

"Wondering what?"

"If...you know, if we could spend time together on the ranch."

"Spend time together? Like how?"

"Out there. You know, I'd love to work with you."

He chuckled. "I don't know if you'd like that."

"And why not? You don't think I could be a good cowgirl?"

"Maybe," he said, arching his sexy brow. "Well, now just what did you have in mind?"

Chapter 15

The following day, Jesse prepared Bella for the cattle drive. He wondered if he'd made a serious mistake.

"So, what do I need?" she asked, innocently, standing in the hallway of his cabin.

She captivated him with those pretty pouty lips of hers. She wore hip-hugging jeans that really accentuated her gorgeous curves. She also wore a t-shirt that flattered her figure.

He grinned, sheepishly. "Well, you'll need a cowboy hat, heeled boots"

"Oh, right. I've got my cowboy boots here. I had my assistant pick them up in town."

He smiled. "Good. Looks like you planned this out well."

"Well, I knew stilettos wouldn't work here for ranch life," she teased him with a grin and a wink.

"Good. I see you also have a pair of riding pants, your jeans."

"Yep. These are comfy." She showed off her ensemble.

"You look good, but you'll need long sleeves."

"Why?"

"To protect you from the sun. And don't forget to put on sunscreen."

"Right. Gotcha."

After they got their ensemble together, she asked. "So what is a cattle drive exactly?"

"Well, it's how we move a herd of cattle from one place to another. We usually guide them on horseback."

"Nice."

"We also have a cattle-drive run for guests so they could get a taste of life on a ranch and see how cowboys live and how things were done back in the old days."

"You mean like in the wild west?"

He grinned. "Life on the ranch is full of hard work, but it's an adventure and it gives you a good workout too."

"I can see that," she said, her eyes grazing him with admiration. He felt heat rise to his chest. He had to keep his focus. But it was hard

"As for cattle runs," he continued. "Like I said, we do it for our guests and we do a short run guiding the cows from one pasture to the next so they can graze on fresh grass."

"Won't they go on their own?"

He chuckled. "Cows don't always go where you want them to. They have a mind of their own. They need guidance. Sometimes we get a team of us cowboys out there to do that, along with a trail boss."

"Good. And let me guess, you're the trail boss today."

"That's right." He put on his cowboy hat.

"Nice. You know, I feel so relaxed here on the ranch. It's a nice escape from the city life, the hustle and bustle of traffic, congestion, fast-living, and crowds. This is just what I need. A breath of fresh air."

"Oh, you'll be getting a lot of that around here."

"I can see why you left the city to come back here. I don't blame you one bit."

"You don't?"

"Nope. I wish I could do this."

"Then why don't you?" Was he boldly asking her to stay with him down here?

She sighed deeply. "I wish. But my life is in front of the camera. And I may get the biggest role of my life soon. If all goes well."

"Right. How was that audition?"

"It went well. At least I think it did. But we'll see..." Her voice trailed off.

He didn't want her thinking too much about her life in Hollywood. She needed a break from all that. And he knew just how to do it.

***

"Hold on," he told her as she held him behind his back.

Feeling her arms around his waist as he rode on the ranch with his other brothers, guiding a herd of cows to the next pasture felt right at home. It was as if she belonged there, right beside him.

"This is fun," she said.

"Glad you like it."

"Talk about adventure."

"Maybe next time, you can ride with us, on your own horse."

"I'd love that."

He could see his brothers Luke and Beau exchanging glances with a smile. He could only guess what they were thinking.

Right now, he was enjoying his time with Bella. Even if it was only going to last for a short time. It wasn't the length of time; it was the depth of it. And he was going to enjoy every second of it.

The air was fresh and the wind blew a gentle breeze as they worked out there in the sun.

Later, Bella did get up on her own horse. And man, did she really take the reins. It was as if she was built for being a cowgirl.

"For someone who's never done this before, you sure know what you're doing?"

"I'm a fast learner. I can get into any role."

He grinned.

"I'm sure you can."

By the end of the session, they'd successfully moved the herd of cows.

Later, they met up at the mess hall for dinner with the other ranch hands. She seemed to fit right in with everyone. She was so friendly and didn't act like an actress. He was glad she fit in okay, and everyone seemed to get on with her.

After dinner, he got up and carried the empty plates back to the kitchen.

"You and Bella are really hitting it off," Billy, their cook, said while wiping down the countertop.

"She's a real trooper," Jesse agreed.

"Shame about what John did to her."

"I know." It boiled his blood just thinking about it. "But that's the past now."

"You two serious?" Billy asked.

Jesse didn't know how much to tell him. He and his brothers knew they had to be married off soon, but they didn't tell everyone what was going on. And right now he would leave it at that.

"Maybe," Jesse said, with a grin.

He knew it wouldn't last long. But he could not get her curves out of his mind. He loved it when she put her arms around his waist as they rode the horse together while they guided the cattle earlier. He didn't want her to ride alone for the first time. It could get crazy out there. But she was all right in managing herself.

Gosh, he admired her. He admired every inch of her.

But a little voice inside told him, not to get too attached. It would all be over soon. Could this last? Would she change her mind and stay with him?

Chapter 16

The following week, Bella sat nervously in the limo. Jesse sat by her side on the plush leather seat.

"Relax, you'll be fine." He gave her a good hug and squeeze and all of a sudden, his energies relaxed her.

"I will."

"So you've got two awards to give out?" he asked.

"No. I have to present one award. Then I'm scheduled to accept my father's lifetime achievement award."

"Nice. You can do it, Bella. I believe in you."

And with those words, his reassuring eyes and voice, she felt she could do this.

Jesse looked stunning in his gorgeous tux and cowboy hat. She loved that look. She wore a black, beaded evening gown for the occasion and her hairdo in an updo off her face.

Jesse told her earlier that her look really accentuated her features.

"Thank you," she said, softly.

The *Dallas Academy of Film and TV Awards* show was only moments away now. She'd be facing the press and all her industry associates. And she'd be facing Olson James, the famous director, and John and his new bride to be, A-list actress, Alexis.

The limo pulled up and immediately the noise from the crowds and the photographers drowned them out.

There were screams and shouts from the crowd as she and Jesse stepped out of the limo and they walked the red carpet like a loving couple.

"Bella! Bella!" She heard the crowd scream out her name.

For the first time she felt right at home. And she thanked Jesse for making it possible. She couldn't imagine turning up there alone after what John did to her and knowing he would be there with Alexis, after dumping her so publicly.

Jesse protected her so she wouldn't have to answer any media questions and before long they were in the auditorium.

She looked around but didn't see Olson James. Her agent Moss sat at her table. She introduced Jesse to Moss and his date for the evening. She could feel the glares and stares from everyone in the auditorium.

Someone had asked her earlier if she'd like to be seated far away from John and Alexis, but she told them it didn't matter. And she meant it.

"Well, you're up soon," Moss told her, later in the ceremony.

Bella drew in a deep breath.

Jesse squeezed her hand under the table.

"You can do it," he whispered to her, his beautiful brown eyes capturing hers and her heart turned over in her chest.

She could do this. Especially with Jesse at her side.

She then spotted James the producer/director in the front row. She got up and went to the stage, her new stilettos were killing her feet, but she'd manage. When she got to the stage, she kept looking at Jesse and pretending he was the only one she was speaking to.

"And the award goes to..." She opened the envelope. "Liam Green, for Chile Sauce: The Movie."

A round of applause erupted and she held her smile and confidence.

Later, she gracefully accepted the award for her father. The night was turning out better than she'd expected, all the while, her handsome cowboy cheering her on.

But when she went to leave the stage, she tripped on her long gown and went down like a bale of hay.

Gasps could be heard all around her.

This was a disaster. She heard laughter erupt in the audience. But she didn't care. She was utterly humiliated.

She could imagine the media would say now: *Actress falls apart at awards show.*

Her ex-fiancé and his new fiancée were there, watching. Cameras rolled. Olson James, the director witnessed all what was happening.

She'd messed up big time. This was supposed to be her big comeback, but there was no coming back from that now.

Then...

She felt the arms around her and that wonderful cologne scent. It was sweet Jesse.

He'd helped her up. But it was too late, she was down. Down in the dumps. She could never recover from this humiliation. And she could kiss her future role in that new rom-com goodbye.

Chapter 17

Jesse held onto Bella behind the stage, her agent, Moss, approached them, frantic.

"Let's go," Moss said. "You don't have to show up at the after party."

"She's not going anywhere," Jesse said.

"What?" Bella turned to Jesse, surprised.

"So what if you fell?" Jesse said, comforting her. "People fall. It's just like riding a horse, you get back up, you don't lie in the dirt waiting to get run over."

She looked at him, stunned. He didn't mean to be so hard on her, but it was for her own good.

"There's no way you're going to let them have the last laugh, Bella. Remember what we spoke about last week? About that philosophical saying?"

"Oh, no. You're talking about philosophy now?" Moss said.

Jesse looked at Moss and arched his brow, then he returned his attention back to Bella. "Our greatest glory is not in never falling."

"But getting up every time we fall," she completed the saying.

"Atta, girl," Jesse said. "You should show them what you're made of. Dust yourself off and get back on stage."

She sprung to her feet, her assistant by her side. Jesse holding her up.

"How bad is it?" Jesse asked her. "How's your ankle?"

"Just a little twist, it's okay. I think my pride was more hurt." She grinned.

He liked that he could get her to smile again. It meant a lot to him to see her okay. There was no way he was letting her lose out on this battle.

She sucked in a deep breath and she broke free from them and got back to the side of the stage. She spoke to the stage director and whispered something to him. The show was still going on, thankfully.

But he didn't hear what sort of arrangement was made.

It turned out that there was a slip of paper on the stage and when her heel went over it, it caused her to slide. Luckily, she was all right. Now, she just had to make sure her reputation stayed in tack.

He didn't know why but an overwhelming sense to protect her came over him.

Later, she walked back on stage, moving proudly and with an air of confidence.

Bella kicked off her heels and told the crowd, "You know, I don't need heels to feel tall. I'm already this big." She grinned widely. "Now, let's do this right, without tripping up."

Her smile was wide as the ocean and the crowd went nuts, everybody clapped and cheered her on.

And she gave another version of the acceptance speech and walked off the stage proudly with her father's award, bowing graciously and smiling.

Everyone stood up and gave her a standing ovation.

Pride swelled up inside of Jesse. He was so proud of her.

"You nailed it, girl," Jesse said to Bella later.

"Thanks, Jesse. I couldn't have done it without you."

"Oh, you could have. Sometimes we all need a little encouragement. Nothing wrong with that."

***

Later, Bella and Jesse rode in the limo back to the ranch, photographers tried to get a snapshot of her, but the windows were tinted.

Just then her agent called her on her cell phone.

She answered it.

When she got off the phone, she looked lost.

"Something wrong?"

"I don't believe it," Bella said, looking dazed.

"What's wrong?" Concern washed over Jesse.

Did someone say something to upset his pretty fiancée?

Chapter 18

"I got the part!" Bella said, not believing it. She sat dazed in the limo as they headed back to the ranch.

"What? You got the role in that new romantic comedy?"

"Yes. The director spoke to Moss after we left. He told Moss that he admired my guts and courage for getting back on stage after that fall and I'm the type of actress he wants to work with for his new role." She squealed with delight, hardly containing herself.

"Wow! I don't know what to say."

"Oh, my gosh! This is happening so fast." Her heart beat as fast as her thoughts. "I can't believe this is really happening."

She leaned over and hugged Jesse and he hugged her back. She enjoyed the feel of his warmth and his loving touch.

"Thanks to you, Jesse. I don't know how to thank you."

"For what? You did it all, girl."

"No, but you encouraged me. You gave me a place to relax and rejuvenate after all this fiasco and then you were there for me when I fell on stage."

"Glad I was there at the right time."

Yes, at the right time. The Lord placed Jesse in her life at the right time.

Her father always told her that when one door closed another would open up, but we get so focused on the closed door that we don't always see what door the Lord opens up for us.

Well, she knew now.

She was down about her ex before, but not now. Not anymore. She was glad to have Jesse in her life and now her career was back on track.

This was her comeback.

The director told Moss that because Bella got back up and showed pride. That showed class. Real class. She thought about it. Two million dollars for her role would pay off all her father's medical bills, buy a house cash, and be on her way.

"Congratulations, darling. I'm so happy for you. It's what you've always wanted."

"It is, Jesse. You have no idea."

"So will they be filming here in Texas?"

Her heart sank. She just realized what he'd asked.

"Oh, no."

"What's wrong?" he asked, concerned.

"Jesse, I...I'll have to leave Texas. I can't be in Sweet Rivers while they're filming."

"Oh." His tone was filled with disappointment and that made her heart ache.

This handsome kind cowboy had done so much for her. And now she'd have to leave him.

"We can still get married. Oh, don't worry about that. We made an arrangement, and I'm going to see it through. It's just that, well...my agent said I'll need to be out there on Monday."

"Monday? That's two days away."

"I know. Let's get married tomorrow. It's a good thing you got the marriage licence last week. So we can get married on Sunday. Then I'll leave on Monday evening. That'll give us a full day and night together."

That way, his lawyer would think they at least consummated their marriage, though they both knew deep down it was only a fake marriage.

He didn't say anything for a while. He just leaned back in the plush leather seat of the limo, looking out the window as they headed back to Sweet Rivers.

Had she offended him?

Wasn't he happy for her?

Chapter 19

Jesse was crushed.

So Bella was leaving him?

This was how it was all going to end?

They'd finally arrived home and he'd walked her to her room before heading back downstairs to the kitchen to fix himself a drink.

He could not believe this.

The ride in the limo was quiet after she announced she would be moving back to the west coast.

A part of him felt terrible for not showing more enthusiasm. He was happy for her. So what happened?

She told him she'd keep in touch and then when it was time to end their marriage she'd be back in town.

But he knew how long-distance relationships were, even fake ones. Distance could really put a wedge between them.

There would be no more cattle drives, or horseback rides together into the sunset on the ranch. No more eating dinner together in the cabin and taking a walk on the grounds of the ranch. No more going to church together on Sunday mornings. No more time together.

He knew they'd be married for convenience's sake, but there was a small part of him that hoped, prayed that she'd get closer to him while they lived together under the same roof pretending to be a married couple. Just like his brother Luke and his new bride, Jemma. And Beau and his new bride Lucky.

Speaking of luck.

It didn't look as if he'd be that lucky. A day after the wedding he'd be driving his new bride to the airport. And that would be the end of it.

And the end of whatever hope he had of making their convenient marriage real.

Chapter 20

Bella couldn't believe the day had arrived.

It was Sunday. Her quickie wedding day to Jesse Carsen would happen any moment now. She'd barely slept a wink last night, thinking of today and how fast things were moving in her life. But it was for the best.

She stood there on the make-do-altar on the ranch, facing her handsome cowboy and looked deeply into his loving eyes.

It was their wedding day, yet she knew that tomorrow she would not be enjoying her fake honeymoon with charming, fun-to-be-with Jesse. She would be alone on a flight back to the west coast for her new role. Could she do this?

She had to. This was her life now. Her dream. She could always come back between movies and visit him. She didn't want to lose their friendship.

Lizzy, as promised, was her maid of honor. She was so glad she could make it at such short notice.

Jesse had previously gotten the marriage license when they'd decided to go for the marriage of convenience, so it was convenient that Pastor Dave said he'd marry them after service today, on the ranch.

It was a small intimate occasion. And they'd hired a photographer. She wanted it to be private like most Hollywood weddings these days. Out there with nature and the warmth of the sun shining down on them.

"You may now kiss the bride," Pastor Dave said after at the end of the marriage vows. And Jesse leaned down and pressed his sweet lips to hers, capturing her with his softness.

And oh, someone catch her, she felt as if her knees would buckle down any moment now.

This cowboy could kiss!

His lips were so soft and pleasurable. She felt butterflies tickle her belly as he held her so lovingly.

How could this be fake?

She thought this was supposed to be a fake arranged marriage. Yet, what she felt was so real.

How could this be?

She was going to miss him. She was going to miss her sweet, handsome, and caring cowboy.

When he pulled his lips away, everyone cheered and clapped, and the music started playing again.

She was breathless.

"Are you all right, my darling bride?" he said, still holding her.

"Yes. I...you stole my breath away," she whispered to him.

She saw the loving look in his eyes, yet it was tainted with a bit of sadness. She knew why.

She caused it, didn't she? She was leaving him.

But it had to be this way. He'd understand later, wouldn't he?

Besides, he would have what he needed to stay on the ranch as per his late father's will, and she'd have what she wanted. Her reputation in Hollywood back intact after that humiliating public dumping by her Hollywood actor ex-fiancé.

But that was the past now. This was the present.

Later, they danced in the hall at the main lodge and everyone seemed so jovial. The atmosphere was electric. The photographer snapped away capturing their pretend wedding and she felt something inside. She had no idea what. But her eyes never left her handsome cowboy husband.

A husband she'd have for only one year, while she worked in Hollywood.

Chapter 21

That kiss.

Jesse stared up at the ceiling in the dark while he lay in bed on Monday night, thinking of his wedding on Sunday.

Bella's lips felt like a sweet angelic kiss to his soul. His body felt alive with all kinds of emotions. He missed her. He missed her presence, her beauty, her touch. He missed her deeply. So deep, it hurt to his core.

And that was the first and last kiss he'd ever have with her. Emotions climbed up inside him.

She called him earlier when she arrived in L.A. to let him know she was all right.

He was glad at least *one* of them was all right, because he sure wasn't.

His new wife was 1,436 miles away from him. Yep, that's right. He measured the distance between them on the map.

It would be a twenty-hour drive if he wanted to drive out there to see her, or a three-hour flight.

Man, he missed her like crazy. And she was so far away.

Jesse couldn't believe that kiss yesterday. His wedding to Bella Lovely. They would stay married for a year while she lived in Hollywood and it crushed him inside to have that distance between them.

He prayed to the Lord to give him strength to get through this. He never thought he'd ever fall in love given his past. His ex had left him because he was so distant. And look at the irony of his fake marriage now.

He'd taken her to the airport earlier and now he was in bed, by himself.

They'd slept in separate rooms yesterday, of course. That was the arrangement, right? But it felt so wrong.

He should have been with his bride in every sense of the word.

That's probably why they say be careful what you wish for because you just might get it. And be sorry for it.

Well, he sure was now. He was sorry he wished for a convenient bride to fulfil his adoptive father's last wishes. Because that's what he got, and it hurt that they couldn't be a real married couple now.

***

Later, in the night, there was a sound coming from downstairs that woke Jesse up.

He reached for his cell phone at his side table and saw the display on his phone read 4:00 a.m.

He slept on and off during the night. He was planning to rise about 5:00 a.m. to get ready to feed the cows, but now he was awake an hour earlier than he'd intended.

Then...

He heard the sound again.

Was someone breaking into his cabin?

He sprung up out of bed and put on his jeans then turned on the light. He also turned on the light on the landing upstairs.

"Who's there?" he called out, boldly.

He wondered if one of his brothers decided to pay him a prank visit.

They'd commented to him yesterday after the service how much he looked depressed and could use some cheering up.

They figured he felt down about Bella having to leave town so soon. But she was in Hollywood now, wasn't she? All the way on the west coast.

He then made his way downstairs but then he stopped, and his breath caught in his throat. His eyes could not believe what he was seeing.

It was Bella.

"Bella? What are you doing here, darling?"

Was he dreaming?

He must be dreaming.

He had to be.

He was hallucinating.

Bella was in Hollywood now.

"I'm here." Her large pretty brown eyes gazed lovingly into his. He went down to her to see if she was really there.

And she hugged him tightly. He returned the hug, feeling her warmth, her love.

"I thought you left?" he said to her, the pretty floral scent of her perfume filled the air between them.

"I couldn't stay," she said, breathless as if she'd just finished running a marathon. "I had to come back here."

"But...what about your role of a lifetime in that movie?"

"I haven't signed the contract yet. I was supposed to sign it when I got there. But it was a good thing I didn't because I already have the role of a lifetime," she said to him.

She wrapped her arms around him and gazed lovingly into his eyes.

"I don't get it," he said.

"*This* is my role of a lifetime," she said, breathlessly. "As your loving wife. I don't want Hollywood, cowboy. I want you."

"Oh, darling. I want you too. But I want you to follow your dream. I thought you wanted the role in that movie."

"I thought so too. But I felt depressed when I got there. I only took the role because I thought it would make me happy, but it didn't. I felt empty there. Hollywood doesn't feel the same to me as it did in the past. I guess I've changed. As it turns out, the director's niece also auditioned for the part and she wanted it more than I do, so everyone's happy. I feel so amazing when we're together. I don't want to spend a day or a week or a month without you. Life's too short for that. And I've seen what can happen to long-distance relationships—especially in Hollywood. I want you, Jesse. All of you."

A smile curved his lips, and emotion welled up inside of him as he embraced her closer.

"Oh, darling, I want you too. More than you'll ever know."

And with those words, he brushed his lips against hers passionately and lovingly sealed their marriage with a kiss to cherish for a lifetime.

***

Thank you for reading *Her Fake Fiancé Cowboy*. Those Carsen brothers are really something, aren't they? Will Chase find true love again? Read book four in the Carsen Brothers of Sweet Rivers Ranch available soon!

***

For more information on sweet romances that fill your heart with joy, or to sign up for updates on new releases, you can send a message to Marie Richards at pageturningstories@gmail.com She loves to hear from readers.